Desert Slam

Steven Barwin

orca soundings

ORCA BO

Library and Archives Canada Cataloguing in Publication

Barwin, Steven, author
Desert slam / Steven Barwin.
(Orca soundings)

Issued in print and electronic formats.
ISBN 978-1-4598-1372-4 (paperback).—ISBN 978-1-4598-1373-1 (pdf).—
ISBN 978-1-4598-1374-8 (epub)

I. Title. II. Series: Orca soundings
PS8553.A7836D48 2017   jc813'.54   C2016-904453-X
C2016-904454-8

First published in the United States, 2017
Library of Congress Control Number: 2016950088

Summary: In this high-interest novel for teen readers, Maya is
involved in a car accident while on vacation in Palm Springs.

MIX
Paper from
responsible sources
FSC® C016245

*Orca Book Publishers is dedicated to preserving the environment and has
printed this book on Forest Stewardship Council® certified paper.*

Orca Book Publishers gratefully acknowledges the support for its
publishing programs provided by the following agencies: the Government
of Canada through the Canada Book Fund and the Canada Council
for the Arts, and the Province of British Columbia through
the BC Arts Council and the Book Publishing Tax Credit.

Cover image by iStock.com

ORCA BOOK PUBLISHERS
www.orcabook.com

Printed and bound in Canada.

20 19 18 17 • 4 3 2 1

To my family

Chapter One

Small white wind turbines dotted the desert terrain. Leaning against the curved wall of the airplane, I felt the vibrations travel through me and heard the accompanying clanking sound as the wheels dropped. My excitement over landing in Palm Desert, California, one of my favorite places in the world, made me want to unbuckle and dance around.

I pressed my face against the window to take it all in. The desert mountains came into view as we made a sweeping turn to land.

My stomach lurched as we descended, and my ears popped. It wouldn't be long now.

The airplane door opened and everyone got in line to get off, anxious to see the blue skies and feel the dry heat.

Inside the terminal, I yanked my suitcase off the carousel and stepped through the sliding doors into paradise. I adjusted my sunglasses and guided my suitcase wheels onto the curb. I took in a deep breath of the dry desert air. A double honk caught my attention. I smiled and waved as Grandpa John pulled up in his sky-blue convertible. After some hugs and kisses we hit the road.

"So how's my favorite grand-daughter?" he asked as he pulled onto a highway flanked by desert on either side.

"Your one and only granddaughter," I said. The sky was the most perfect, spotless blue. I couldn't resist. I used my phone to snap my first picture of the trip. "I'm great. So excited to see you guys and to play and watch lots of tennis too."

"Speaking of tennis, all the hotels are sold out for the Indian Wells tournament. This place gets busier than Times Square on New Year's Eve."

"That's because it's one of the best tournaments on tour," I replied.

"Can't argue with you there."

We didn't speak for a few minutes. I was just enjoying the warm air rushing past me, blowing my hair straight back like a wave.

"So I heard you're a full-fledged driver now," my grandpa finally said. "Congratulations!"

"Thank you. I am officially a free woman. The open road is calling to me."

He smiled at me, and his sunglasses reflected my face. "All you need is a car."

I laughed. "That would help. Where's Granny Evelyn?"

"Home. Unfortunately, her back is out again. Slipped disk is acting up."

"Oh no. She's not golfing?"

"Not for at least another week. She's kind of going crazy at home. All she can do is watch others play from the balcony."

We turned off the highway and onto a road lined with palm trees. I snapped another photo. The gates parted and let us into the Tuscan Palms community. I sighed, all the tension from life in busy Vancouver draining from my body as we entered golf, tennis and swimming heaven. I dragged my suitcase up to the second-floor condo. Inside, the walls were painted in bright tropical colors. There was a hint of coconut sunblock in the air.

Perfect.

I propped my suitcase and tennis-racket bag on the bed in the guest room.

Granny Evelyn called out, "You're here!"

I found her on the balcony, stretched out in a chair with a book. "Don't get up," I said, giving her an extra-long hug.

"How was the flight?"

"Good. Are you okay?" I asked, even though I knew the answer by the way she grimaced whenever she moved.

"I will be. But who can complain with this view?"

She was right. Beyond the balcony was the golf course—the eighth hole stretched out in front of us. A golfer stepped to his fairway ball, lowered his club in front of it and waggled his butt before swinging.

"It's a great sport," Grandpa John said. "I think you'd be good at it."

The golf ball jumped ahead and to the left and was swallowed by a small pond.

The golfer smashed his club into the grass.

"Sorry, I just don't get it," I said.

"That's okay. Someone famous once said that *golf is a good walk spoiled*," Grandpa John said.

My grandmother jumped in. "Don't knock it!"

"Thank you for inviting me down for March break."

"We told you—the invitation is always open. Everything good in Vancouver?"

I gave her the update, even though I spoke with her and Grandpa John every Sunday night. "I can't wait to hit the tennis court."

"Well, you're only here for a week," she said. "Go have fun. It's hot out there, so take lots of water."

I nodded and got changed.

At the door, Grandpa John was waiting for me. He held out a key and a plastic electronic key pass attached to a palm-tree keychain. "This'll get you through the gates, and this one's for the condo." He put that key in the lock and checked it before handing it to me.

I opened the large gate by swiping the pass and stepped into the tennis area. Tall palm trees lined perfectly green courts with bright white borders. There looked to be six courts, and they were all empty. You have them all to yourself, I thought. I chose court three because over the fence and beyond the palms I could see the mountains.

With no pressure and no rush, I lined up my tennis balls on the ground for serve practice.

I chose one and bounced it repeatedly on the baseline, catching it in my left hand each time. The complete silence except for the occasional bird actually made it harder to focus. So I filled it with imaginary chatter from a nonexistent crowd. Then I grasped the yellow tennis ball and tossed it gently into the air. At the top of its arc I reached up, fully extended, and thwacked the ball. On my follow-through I watched it soar over the net and land deep in the left service court, just before no-man's-land.

After six serves I stopped for a water break, already in a full sweat.

On the far side of the court I gathered my stray tennis balls and set up to serve again. With wins at Wimbledon, and the French and Australia Opens behind me, this serve could get me the US Open and make me the youngest Grand Slam winner in tennis history.

Three bounces, and then I sent the ball into the air and smacked it hard and with spin, finding the sweet spot. It touched down where the singles sideline met the service line.

"An ace!" I called out, raising my racket in the air. At center court I took a bow and blew kisses to my fans.

"Nice serve."

I turned to see a girl of about my age and height. Caught off guard, I stuttered a hello.

"You must really be a tennis fan to be out here in the heat," she said.

I nodded. "My parents call it an addiction."

"Same here. Only my parents call it HTF—hardcore tennis fan. I'm Ruby."

"Maya."

"Want to play?"

I nodded. "Love to."

We took our sides, and Ruby served first. She was good enough to keep me on my toes. And once the ball was in motion, our rallies were so epic that we needed water breaks after each one.

"This was perfect," Ruby said after we finished. "Just what I needed.

Right now my friends are in a deep freeze." She pointed to her knees. "Snow up to here in Brooklyn."

"In Vancouver we hardly ever get any snow. Only rain. And lots of it. It never gets very cold, but there aren't any palm trees or anything."

"Yeah, this place is a nice break from having to deal with weather. Blue skies every single day."

"Are you here alone?" I asked.

"No, I'm here with my brother. He's younger and totally annoying."

"How about another game tomorrow?"

"Sounds great. Maybe early morning so it's not a hundred degrees."

I laughed. "Good idea."

We exchanged numbers and said our goodbyes, and I walked back to the condo, my clothes stuck to me like a second skin. The condo air conditioning washed over me, and it felt good, like I was hugging a brick of ice. My shower started off cold, and I gradually increased the heat as my temperature returned to normal. Changed, wet hair in a ponytail, I felt brand-new.

On the balcony, my grandparents were sipping wine and snacking on peanuts and pretzels. "How was it?" my grandmother asked.

I took a seat on a white chair. "It was great. I met a girl named Ruby, and we played a few sets."

Grandpa John held out a blue plastic cup. "Lemon-lime sparkling soda water."

"Yes, please." It was calm and quiet outside. Beyond the perfectly manicured grass, the sun was on its way down. To the right was a still pond.

"Isn't that pond beautiful? Those tall green leaves are called mare's tails. And around the edge are water violets."

"Beautiful, like a painting," I agreed. In the distance was a mountain range, almost too perfect to be real. I took a picture and made it my new wallpaper.

"So about dinners," my grandmother said. "We need to plan out our meals, because restaurants will get busy with the tennis tournament going on. There's the clubhouse, which is always good, plus M Kitchen for your favorite ahi tuna burgers."

"And Los Sushi," I added.

"We already have reservations for that Friday night," my grandfather said, sipping his wine.

My grandmother nodded. "And because we will be going out so much, I'm preparing chicken parmesan for tonight."

"Only if I can help."

"Only if you want. You're on vacation."

"Yes, I want to." I nodded. "I know I still have to graduate, go to college, turn tennis pro and tour the world, but I can get used to the retired life. Super jealous."

They smiled. "Oh," my grandfather said, sitting up in his chair. "We have a surprise for you."

I sat up too.

"We heard you were having trouble getting these, and it just so happens there was a charity auction and I was the highest bidder. How does dinner court-side sound?"

"That a new restaurant?"

"No. It's the Indian Wells Tennis Garden."

I was confused. He handed me an envelope, and I opened it. "What? No!" I pulled out tickets for the BNP Paribas Open. "We're going to the tournament?" I cried. I was jumping up and down and making enough noise to destroy the peaceful ambiance for anyone around.

Chapter Two

I had never had a reason this good to get up so early in the morning. Most of the world was still asleep, and Ruby and I were already in our second set.

"Your game is really in the zone," she said from across the court.

"Thanks. My serves are landing deep, and my shot has lots of spin. I think it's just being here, you know? Sunshine, no wind, just perfect conditions."

"You're saying it's the weather— I'm saying it's you!"

"That's very nice of you."

We split two more games, both tie-breakers, until it got way too hot and we were too sweaty to be running around anymore. On our way out the gate and back to the condos, Ruby asked, "Are you interested in coming by to my *grand-mère*'s condo after dinner to watch some of the tennis on TV? My whole family is really into it."

"I'd love to, but I can't tonight." I didn't want to just come out and tell her I was going to the actual game, because that would make her jealous, and I didn't want her to think I was a show-off.

"Okay, maybe another time."

We moved past the pool and across a small street. It looked so hot, you could probably cook breakfast on it. "Actually, the reason I'm unavailable tonight is because my grandparents got tickets for the Indian Wells tennis tournament."

"Really? Wow. I wouldn't come over and watch it on TV either!"

"I'm sorry. I appreciate the invite."

"Don't be. Seriously. You'll have to tell me all about it tomorrow."

"Sounds good."

After some time in the pool and a little nap following an attempt to read a book, it was finally time to go. My grandfather and I walked slowly to the car to keep pace with my grandmother. I was wondering if she'd need a wheelchair to get around at the game. We finally made it to the car, me doing a terrible job of containing my excitement.

The doors unlocked, and I opened the front passenger door for my grandmother.

She moved toward the car, then paused.

"Everything okay?" I asked.

She looked at me, both hands resting above the door. "It hurts too much to bend down to get in. I'm sorry."

I gave her a long hug. "It's okay." I helped guide her away from the car.

We got her back upstairs and sitting comfortably in a chair. I was really worried about her, and I felt bad leaving her, but she insisted we get a move on.

"Go, go—I don't want you to be even later. Just sell my ticket at the gate."

I already had someone in mind.

Back at the car, my grandfather held up the keys. "How'd you like to do the honors?"

I was a little nervous, but I jumped at the opportunity. I steered the convertible through the streets of the gated community.

"There's 3109 on the left."

I pulled over and waved to Ruby.

She jumped in the back. "Thank you so much inviting me!"

"We're happy you could join us," my grandfather said. "Okay, Maya, you're doing great. Outside the main gate you're going to want to turn left."

Driving through the streets of Palm Desert was easy, thanks to the glow-in-the-dark cat's-eyes lining the road. If I were in the wrong lane, I'd feel them against the tires. We crossed over into Indian Wells, and the tennis stadium came into view like a beacon. We parked and made our way past TV news vans with giant satellite dishes on them. After standing in a small lineup we entered through a white picketed security fence. Past the main gate, palm trees lined the way to the tennis courts. Ruby and I practically skipped the entire way.

We passed a man wearing a crazy tennis-ball costume.

"We need to take a picture!" I said. Ruby asked him if he'd mind and then we stood on either side of him while Grandpa John took a photo.

We continued on, and Ruby said, "This place is like its own city," pointing at restaurants, tennis shops and countless lemonade stands.

We paused at a large video wall outside a tented area. It had all the main matches on. "We have tickets, guys," I said. "If we were going to watch tennis here, we might as well be at home!"

I took the steps two at a time through our gate entrance. I stopped at the landing, taking in the expansive sight ahead of me. The tennis court played center stage to a magnificent view. The blue court was divided into eight parts by crisp white lines. The stands rose steeply, dotted by pixelated people, toward towering lights. Beyond them was that sharp mountain zigzag across the perfect painted sky.

"This is beyond beautiful," Ruby said.

I held up my phone and took a picture. "Favorite new wallpaper."

The crowd started to cheer, and down at courtside I saw the players appear.

I took my grandfather's hand and led him to our seats. "Wow. Have I told you how much I love you, Grandpa John?"

He smiled, and I lined up the three of us for a selfie or two before we sat down.

After some applause the match started, and the crowd was silent. Nothing but the guttural grunts of the women giving their all in each contact with the ball.

I took tons of photos and videos so that when I got home and back to the usual routine, I'd be able to remember everything, from their footwork to their shots. The level of play was better than anything I'd expected. I also aimed my phone at the stadium and surrounding mountains, taking a couple of panoramic shots. I threw in some shameless selfies too, so I could remember what it was like to be here. I wanted to remember how happy I was.

Game, set and match came much too quickly. We hung around the Indian Wells Tennis Garden, did some wishful window-shopping and waited in line for an hour to get a tennis ball signed from someone I'd never heard of. By the time we got back to the car, we were all over-tired, held together by too much Pepsi, deep-fried fish tacos and the adrenaline of overexcitement.

"You okay to drive?" my grandfather asked, buckling in.

"Yeah, if you're okay with it."

He smiled. "Take us home."

I snaked my way through the packed parking lot. It felt like it took forever, and I silently cheered when I was up to make my turn out of there.

"This guy will let you in," Grandpa John said, pointing.

I edged forward cautiously and slid into the heavy traffic leaving the stadium. Police were out, stopping, starting and waving at people.

"You okay?" my grandpa asked, patting my shoulder.

"Not really!"

"You're doing just fine. I told you this town goes tennis nuts."

"What about you, Ruby?" I asked, taking a quick peek in the rearview mirror.

She let out a burst of laughter. "I'm from Brooklyn. In New York we don't drive. We walk and take buses and the subway."

I scanned the bumper-to-bumper traffic and didn't relax my shoulders until we turned onto a side street.

My grandfather said, "This is a little shortcut I know."

The road had a lot less traffic, and I even felt comfortable enough to take a hand off the steering wheel to turn on some music. In the rearview mirror I spotted a car driving very close behind me. He flashed his lights a couple of times, but it wasn't until he honked his horn that my grandfather noticed.

"Just ignore him," he said.

Ruby added, "You're doing the speed limit, so that's his problem."

"I am. Should I pull over?"

"There's only one lane. Just stay where you are," Grandpa John said.

I turned the radio off and gripped the steering wheel tightly. The car continued to stay snugly behind me until it finally found a break in the opposing traffic to shoot around me.

"No offense, Ruby, but American drivers are scary."

"Don't think it's American. I think it's just called being a jerk. And jerks are everywhere."

I laughed. Then a set of double red lights flashed in front of me. I pressed down hard on the brake and saw the car in front of me starting to fishtail.

"Look out!" Grandpa John yelled.

My eyes widened. My right leg was fully extended, the brake pedal pushed all the way to the floor. I didn't think I was going to be able to stop in time.

Screech!

I looked to swerve left, but there was an oncoming car blocking me. So I jerked the steering wheel full right, hoping to jump the curb and miss any trees, hydrants or other obstacles. It was too late. "I can't stop!"

Brace…

The front of my grandfather's car slammed into the back of the car in front of me. The cars connected with brute force.

Silence.

Chapter Three

My neck jolted forward as the seat belt locked. I looked up slowly, squinting over the steering wheel. Our two cars were joined as one.

My grandfather's voice broke the sudden silence. "Everyone all right?"

Until he spoke, I'd almost forgotten I wasn't alone in the car. I did a quick scan and discovered two things. First, Ruby and my grandfather both seemed okay. Second, I could move my back and neck, and that meant I was okay too.

I opened my door and stepped out. We quickly confirmed that we were each all in one piece, but I couldn't stop my hands from shaking.

The man in the other vehicle approached us. He was unshaven, in jeans, a T-shirt and baseball hat. He didn't look older than twenty-something. "That guy in front of me was a total jerk. He just stopped out of nowhere and then took off. Is everyone okay?"

My grandfather said, "We think so."

"Good." He looked back at his car before returning his focus to us. "Now, I admit that I was driving a little too fast behind you, but—" The man moved to the passenger seat of his car, opened the door and leaned in.

I whispered to my grandfather, "It's his fault, right?"

"Well, if he was cut off…"

I was already feeling like a total loser, a complete screwup, when he helped a woman out of the car—a clearly pregnant one. My hands rushed to cover my face. I was praying, cursing and muttering to myself. I felt a hand on my shoulder, but it did very little to help.

They approached.

My grandfather spoke for me. "Are you okay, miss?"

She said, "I think so" with one hand on her belly and the other on her back. "It's my fault he was speeding. I wasn't feeling well, and he was rushing to get me home."

Oh my god, I kept thinking, over and over. The flashing lights of a tow truck appeared. It pulled in front of us. A driver stepped out. "Everything all right here, folks?"

"Not sure," my grandfather responded.

The man turned to the pregnant woman. "Let me call 9-1-1."

"No, I'm okay."

"But I think you should go to the hospital to be safe."

She looked at us. "This is our first. He's just nervous. I really am okay."

"So what should we do?" the man in the other car asked. "Exchange information?"

My grandfather nodded. "Good idea."

They exchanged insurance and phone numbers.

The guy asked, "You a new driver?"

I nodded.

"That sucks." He offered a small smile. "I'm sorry."

The woman placed her hand on her hip. "I just want to go home and lie down."

I hit a car that had a pregnant lady inside! "I'm so sorry about this. How far along are you?"

"Just a few months. Second trimester."

My grandfather returned with his insurance details plus a pen and piece of paper. "Are you sure you don't want to get your wife to a hospital?"

She held her hand up. "I'm okay."

"My name's Dale," the man said. "I noticed your plate isn't from around here."

"Canada. We're down for the winter," my grandfather explained.

The tow-truck driver lifted his baseball hat and scratched his head. "I've heard a lot of hellish insurance stories."

Dale said, "Yeah, but the damage doesn't seem to be too bad. The cars look drivable."

"Not yours," the tow-truck driver said. "Your back fender is pushing in against the wheel."

"It gets worse if we get the police involved. I'm just saying, and only if

you want to, what about settling it here?"
He smiled. "Then we can all go home."

The woman held her belly and announced her discomfort again.

She went to sit on the curb, and my grandfather gave her a hand. "I'm not against settling this, but promise you'll get her to a doctor."

Dale nodded. "Absolutely." He looked at the tow-truck driver. "My dad gave me this car, and this'll just get him mad. Plus, I have a friend who can help fix it." He turned to my grandfather. "Do you have anything on you? Cash?"

My grandfather didn't have to check his wallet. "I only have a couple hundred on me."

The tow-truck driver said, "Look, there's some serious bumper damage, and it could be a lot worse underneath. It might not drive the same after this."

Dale looked anxious. "Let's call it a thousand dollars, and I'll walk away and take my chances."

My grandfather scratched his head. "I don't know. That's pretty steep. Plus, I really am worried about you getting her to a hospital first."

Dale said, "Okay, I guess we run it through insurance then." He looked at the woman and asked, "What do you think?"

She shrugged. "I'm fine. Just settle with them so I can get home."

Dale took her hand and then turned to my grandfather. "What about seven-fifty?" he asked. "There's a gas station about a block from here. They might have a bank machine."

"Okay," said my grandfather. He turned to me. "Then it's over. No awkward questions from the insurance company."

I looked at the cars and the poor pregnant woman and was way too confused to know the right thing to do. I tossed the car keys to my grandfather.

"Maya, you should drive."

"No way!"

"You have to get back behind the wheel."

"Let me think about it," I said—and then sneaked into the backseat. "I'll have lots of time to drive again when I'm home."

My grandfather reluctantly got in to the driver's seat, and we drove to the gas station. He stepped out to get the cash.

In the backseat, I turned to Ruby, who was looking at photos of the accident on her phone. "What are you doing?"

"Sorry," she said and put it away.

"I hope that lady is going to be okay."

"I'm sure she will, Maya."

"How did this go from the best night ever to the worst?"

Ruby placed her hand on mine. "This is just a random incident in the vast universe."

My grandfather came out of the gas station with a white envelope, and we drove back to the scene. The tow truck had hoisted the car up by its front wheels, and I could see the woman sitting in the front seat. My grandfather got out of the car, walked over to Dale and handed him the envelope, then returned to our car. We drove away.

That was it? Done?

Ruby, her hand still on mine, said, "It's all over now."

We drove off in my grandfather's damaged car. All I wanted to do was close my eyes and pretend this was just a nightmare.

I awoke with a headache. Then I remembered. The night before, the car, the crash.

I tried to go back to sleep, but it didn't work. At the side of the curtain where it met the edge of the window I could see sunlight. It was another perfect day in desert paradise for everyone else. I crept around the corner to the breakfast nook, a little embarrassed about seeing my grandfather.

"Good morning," my grandmother called out.

I sat down at the table with her even though I wasn't hungry. "Grandpa still asleep?" I poured a glass of orange juice and spilled it in my absentmindedness.

"Oh no. He was out quite early."

I dabbed at the kitchen table, soaking up orange juice with paper towel. "Where is he?"

"He's taken the car to a repair shop to get a quote on the damages."

I nodded. *Great, I've ruined his vacation too.*

My grandmother scooped up some granola with a spoon. "Please don't feel bad about last night. It can happen to anyone. The important thing is that you're okay. The car is replaceable."

I nodded. I wished I felt that way.

"Here's the important thing. You're on vacation, so your only question should be, what do you want to do today?"

"I'm not sure. I think the only thing I feel like doing is burying my head under my pillow."

"Nonsense. Go have fun."

I stood with no direction or desire. I didn't want to play tennis, because it would only remind me of the previous night.

"At some point, maybe tonight, you should call home and let them know what happened. There are a lot of people here from Vancouver, and word gets around, especially in a condo community like this. Your mom and dad might find out, so it's a whole lot better if it comes from you first."

I nodded.

"But that's tonight. You've got a whole wonderful day ahead of you. Go play tennis, or go to the pool and read, and I'll let you know when he comes home."

Lounging next to the pool, I couldn't calm my mind. The night before, I'd watched some of the best tennis I had ever seen in my life. But now that was overshadowed by what had happened after. Embarrassment didn't even begin to describe how I was feeling. How could I have been so stupid? The pool in front of me and its clear blue water did nothing to improve my mood. The bright yellow sun and its blue background were also wasted on me.

I adjusted my lounger to the lowest notch. Lying back, I closed my eyes. The skidding brakes, my hands strangling the steering wheel and that crunch on impact filled the darkness.

I turned onto my side, as if that would just flick away my thoughts. Flipping over to the other side didn't work either. On my stomach, face squished against the hashed fabric, I focused on my breathing. I loaded up my lungs with a deep breath and let it out slowly through my mouth. A dozen or so times more, and I felt myself drift into a deeper darkness. Finally some quiet.

"Maya."

My eyes popped open. If I'd been asleep, I didn't feel rested. I turned my head and looked up. Blocking the sun was Ruby.

"You okay?"

I turned to a sitting position, feeling hot and dry.

"You're a little burnt." She pointed to my shoulder, then sat down next to me. "I'm guessing you're not in the mood for some tennis."

I shook my head. "Not in the mood for anything."

Chapter Four

"Where are you taking me?"

Ruby looked at me and then back at the road, steering her grandparents' black SUV. She smiled at me. "If I told you, you wouldn't come."

"Did my grandparents put you up to this?"

"Oh no. They would be very upset if they knew."

Ruby steered us toward an outdoor mall set against the mountains.

"I'm not in the mood for shopping."

"We're not."

We parked, and I followed her past a large fountain and up a canopied escalator to the second floor. Ruby finally stopped, leaning against a wall. "Okay, here's the deal. Being worried about the damage to the car is one thing, but that pregnant lady is a whole other thing. You're just like me, Maya. You're not going to stop worrying about her."

"And?"

Ruby held out her phone. "Right after the accident, I took photos. You know, just in case." She flicked past pictures of me from that night, stopping at one of the pregnant woman. She then pinched in closer, past the woman's face to her shirt. "Look."

I read an out-of-focus name tag. "*Plus and—*" It was cut off. Below that were the letters *L-A-U-R*—also cut off.

"I did a quick search for stores with that name and…" Ruby pointed. Across from us was a women's clothing store called Plus and Minus.

"She got hurt. Why would she be working today?"

"Let's ask for her phone number. Then you'll know."

I nodded, and a small smile escaped my lips.

Ruby smiled. "The only way I'm going to get to play tennis before I have to go home is if you start feeling better."

The clothing store had red-brick wallpaper covered in graffiti. On the back wall was a mural of a NYC bridge that made Ruby feel right at home. We circled the inside until a woman asked us if we needed help.

Ruby started with, "Are you the manager?"

The woman nodded, a little perplexed.

"We are looking for someone who works here. I think her name is Lau…" Ruby let the word linger, hoping the woman would fill in the rest.

"Girls, if you're not here to shop, then I have to ask you to leave."

"Maybe Lauren?"

Another worker popped up from behind a rack of fashionable hats. "I think they're looking for Laurie."

"Can we have her number?" I asked.

"I can't give out that information. I'm sorry. Please leave."

"It's okay," I said. "Ruby, let's go."

The hat lady said, "Isn't she working today at two?"

The manager barked back, "Don't you have boxes to unpack?"

We both thanked the lady and left before she called security.

After a couple of window-shopping laps around the mall, I sat down with Ruby, keeping one eye on the store and the other on my iced tea.

"What if she doesn't show?" I asked.

"Yeah, she might not. On the bright side," Ruby said, "we are surrounded by palm trees and blue skies."

I nodded, sipping my drink through a purple straw. "If we do find her, what do you think I should say to her? I mean, other than sorry."

"Ask her how she's feeling. And tell her you're glad she is able to return to work. That must mean the baby and her are doing okay."

"Look at the girl from Brooklyn, always with the positive spin."

"You betcha. There's no other way to live. Oh, look!"

I turned to see the woman from the crash crossing the plaza, heading toward the clothing store.

"Do you see what I'm seeing?" Ruby asked.

"She's walking fine. Doesn't seem to be in any pain."

"Yes. But look closer."

I didn't understand. The woman wore skinny jeans and a tight white blouse. Then I saw it—she didn't have a round belly. "She's not pregnant?"

Ruby's phone was out, and she was shooting video. "Doesn't add up."

I got to my feet.

"Where are you going?" Ruby asked.

"I haven't slept because of her. I need to talk to her, find out what's going on. Maybe *she* needs to apologize to *me*."

"No. We can't just accuse her."

"Why not?" I asked. "I want my grandfather's money back. Then I'm calling the police!"

"Because she'll just deny it. Come up with some story."

"So we just let her go?"

"No," Ruby said, "we just have to figure out a plan. We know where she works. Let's come back prepared."

With my head in a book and my body stretched out on a lounge chair in front of the pool, I looked like I was on vacation. Too bad I didn't feel like it.

Ruby climbed out of the pool and toweled off. "It's so hot. How can you just lie there?"

"Too tired to move," I muttered, putting my book down.

"You didn't sleep any better last night?"

I shook my head. "I close my eyes and the next thing I know, I'm in the accident. Behind the wheel. I see brake lights, but I can't stop. I'm helpless as the car drifts forward." I paused, pushing back a tear. "Then *smash*, and I'm awake."

Ruby sat in front of me, legs folded. "It was very scary, but it also wasn't your fault. What do your grandparents say?"

"Nothing."

"You haven't told them about the nightmares? You should."

"I've ruined their car. I don't need to also ruin their holiday."

"And that girl, Laurie? Pregnant, then not. It's really bugging me."

An older woman stopped in front of us, her wide-brimmed hat blocking the sun. "Are you Evelyn's granddaughter, Maya?"

"Yes."

"I'm her friend Lillian. She told me all about your accident." She smiled behind oversized sunglasses. "This is a small community. Word gets around. You know, the scary thing is that the same thing happened to me."

Ruby turned to her. "Really?"

"This is my friend Ruby," I said.

"Well, I had gone to meet a friend for lunch. It was right after Christmas, and the roads were packed—you know, with all those Boxing Day sales. It's so busy, but it really is the best time to shop. The deals are too good to pass up. Anyway, where was I?"

"The accident," Ruby reminded her.

"Yes. We had a lovely lunch together, and then in the parking lot, this man backed out and stopped, and I went right into him. But let me tell you, it was not my fault."

"You weren't hurt?" Ruby asked.

"No, but he threatened to call the police. The last thing I want is for my insurance rates to go up. The strange thing was that a few weeks later I saw him in Palm Springs. He told me he didn't recognize me, but it was him."

She left, and Ruby said, "See?"

"See what?"

"I'm not sure yet. But something's not right."

I reached for my book. "That's just a random accident."

"You mean a coincidence."

"Ruby, I never figured you as the conspiracy-theory type!"

Another older woman in the pool swam up to us. "You talking car accidents? Hope you don't mind my eavesdropping, but something similar also happened to me."

"Oh, really? What?" Ruby asked.

"Well, this person suddenly stopped and I hit them. I got out and he said an animal just crossed the road. Luckily, I wasn't driving that fast. The damage wasn't too bad. And fortunately for him, a tow truck was right there to help out. People don't know how to drive!" She shook her head and swam away.

Ruby turned to me and said, "Was that a coincidence too, just a random fender bender?" I noticed people talking and looking over at us.

"You keep asking questions, and we're going to be the center of every small, sad story from an elderly driver." I stood, slid into my flip-flops and grabbed my towel. "I'm getting out of here." I moved to the pool gate, and Ruby followed me.

"Maya, I know this all seems pretty weird, but I really do think we are on to something."

A voice called out behind us. "Oh, girls! I overheard what you were talking about—"

An even older lady, hunched over a walker.

"See what I mean? This is too much." I told Ruby to keep walking.

The lady persisted, inching her way toward us. "It happened close to the movie theaters," she called.

"Oh, come on," Ruby said, stopping. "You can't ignore her."

"Why?"

"She's so cute."

I reluctantly followed Ruby back to the lady.

"The driver, out of nowhere, hit the brakes, and then *crash*."

Ruby whispered out of the corner of her mouth, "Be polite," then bent down to get eye level with the woman.

"Just terrible drivers out there," the woman continued. "You can never be too careful."

Ruby said, "I'm sorry to hear you had an accident."

"Anyway, I didn't want to bother you. As long as everyone's okay, you know?"

I nodded. "Uh-huh."

Ruby asked, "Were you okay?"

"Me?" she chuckled. "Oh no, it wasn't me, dear. I've been driving for over fifty years, and I'm proud to say I've never been in an accident. It was the daughter of one of the people who clean my condo. She's about your age."

I looked at Ruby, impatiently tapping my flip-flop.

"The worst part was, there was a pregnant lady in the other car. People should be more careful. Anyway, I've got to get to my Zumba class. Toodle-oo." The lady turned her walker and made her way back across the sidewalk.

"If one's an incident," Ruby asked, "and two's a coincidence…what's three?"

"A pattern," I admitted.

Ruby nodded.

"Then what's four?" I asked.

"Something we need to investigate."

Chapter Five

"Did she say anything else on the phone?"

Ruby put her grandparents' car in *Park*. "Just that she'll be wearing a Los Angeles Lakers hat."

Through the parking lot we approached the Beach Cove Café. It was a regular strip-mall restaurant, decked out in a beach theme. A hostess dressed in Hawaiian shorts asked how many were in our party, and we said we were meeting someone. At an outdoor table under a beach umbrella, we found the Lakers hat.

I asked, "Are you Cristina?"

She smiled and invited us to sit on a bench made out of a surfboard.

Cristina had straight, flowing black hair to below the collar of her blue-jean jacket.

Ruby picked up a menu. "Thank you for meeting us."

"Truthfully, I was a bit nervous about who would show up."

We made quick introductions as a man appeared in a beach outfit. "Can I get you two a drink?"

Cristina held up her colorful drink. "Ice smoothies are great."

We ordered two, and the man said they'd be right out. Then he sat down next to Cristina.

She smiled. "This is my cousin Javier. He's the manager and insisted we meet here. You know, for safety."

I stared at Ruby, her eyes on the menu. "Yeah, you can never be too careful."

She noticed. "Sorry—the menu looks so good."

"It is," Javier agreed. "I'm the manager here, but I'm also a journalism student. So what's your story? You got Cristina's number from someone at the Tuscan Palms retirement community?"

"Yes." I decided not to share that we had to ask around to find her and then interrupted her Zumba class. My drink arrived with a paper umbrella sticking out of a strawberry.

"My mom knows everyone there," Cristina said. "She runs a cleaning service. Her company cleans most of the condos there." She looked at us. "You two must be on vacation?"

"From Vancouver," I said.

"And I'm from New York," Ruby added.

"So you called me because of a car accident?"

We took turns explaining what had happened after the Indian Wells tennis tournament.

I put my half-finished smoothie to the side. "It's a long shot, but we're hoping our accidents are connected. When did yours happen?"

"A month ago. Kind of the same situation as yours. I was so frustrated, because I knew it wasn't my fault. I couldn't sleep."

I leaned forward. "Me too!"

Javier said, "It's been making her crazy. She wanted to hire a lawyer, but she paid them that night, and they disappeared."

"Yeah." I nodded. "Same thing."

Javier kept an eye out on his restaurant. "I told her to let it go. There's nothing to be done."

Ruby cleared her throat. "Well, that's why we're here." She paused and put her fingertips on her temples. "Sorry, brain freeze. This drink is *so* good."

Javier smiled.

Ruby continued, "We heard that there was a pregnant woman in the other car."

"Yes." Christina nodded. "But I don't get why that's important."

Ruby held out her phone, showing Cristina a picture of the woman at the scene of our accident.

"That's her!" Cristina said, excited. She slapped Javier on the arm. "I told you something didn't add up!"

I placed both my hands flat on the table and spoke slowly. "Cristina…that woman…her name is Laurie, and she's *not* pregnant."

"Hold on," Javier said, his journalist side kicking in. "What does this mean, and is there anything you can actually do about it?"

"Well, we don't exactly know," I said. "But this is way too suspicious to be nothing."

Ruby added, "Laurie's a liar, and she's helping to scam people. We want to take her down."

"I understand." Javier nodded. "But based on what I know from journalism class, there's not enough evidence-based information here."

I turned to Cristina. Trying to convince her with her cousin around would be impossible.

Javier pushed back in his chair. "Ruby, other than a photo, you have nothing. This is a long shot."

Cristina nodded.

"And after everything you just went through, I would have thought you'd want to put all of this behind you." Javier continued. He got up from the table and said as he walked way, "The drinks are on me." Cristina followed him.

When we pulled up to the gates to the condo entrance, Ruby asked if I wanted to go for a swim.

"I'm not really in the mood."

Ruby's phone rang. "Hello? Oh, hi…okay. The Desert Hills shopping mall. Okay." She hung up and started backing the car out.

"What's wrong?" I asked.

"You won't believe this. That was Cristina."

"Really!"

"She wants to help us find Laurie."

"And what about her cousin?"

"She didn't say."

We found Cristina waiting for us at the Coffee Bean kiosk.

"Hi. Thanks for meeting me."

"Javier's not here?" I asked, looking around.

"He's a good guy. Just a little over-protective. So where's the store?"

I walked her within view. We could see Laurie folding clothes in the back. Still not pregnant.

"I have an idea," Cristina said, walking quickly toward the store.

We hurried to keep up. "What's your plan?" I asked.

"Simple. Let's go get her!"

"What are you going to say?" asked Ruby.

"It'll come to me when I get there."

Ruby shot a glance at me, but we followed her into the store.

Cristina walked right in. I hid behind her. Ruby had her phone out, camera at the ready.

We were just a few steps in when the mean manager blocked our way. "You two again. I told you that I'd call security. Guess you thought I wasn't serious." She turned to Laurie, now at the cash register. "Call security. Now!"

Laurie looked at us, focusing mostly on me, clearly trying to place me. Then her eyes widened, and she took off to the back.

The manager blocked us, so all three of us scrambled through the front door. Outside, I spotted Laurie veering past a massive potted plant by the outdoor escalators.

"There she is!" Up the escalator steps two at a time, I led the race after her.

Laurie zigzagged between the small carts selling jewelry and cell-phone cases. She made a sharp left down a hallway that emptied into a restaurant.

"Stay on her!" Ruby shouted.

We blew past the hostess and followed the top of Laurie's head as she bobbed past some booths toward the restroom.

Cristina called out, "We got her!"

I creaked the door open slowly and we entered. It was empty. An angry Cristina pushed at the stall doors one by one. The third door didn't budge. It was locked.

Laurie's voice rang out. "What do you want from me?"

"The truth," Ruby responded.

"Well, I'm not coming out!"

Cristina banged on the door with her shoulder. "And we're not leaving."

"You've got the wrong person!"

I asked, "Then why did you run?"

There was no response.

"Whatever," Cristina said. "Let's go, girls." She signaled for us to follow her to the door. She pulled on it, and as it slowly closed, we tiptoed into the first stall. After a few uncomfortable moments of being squished together, we heard Cristina's stall door open.

We poured out all at once. Laurie let out a scream as Cristina blocked the exit.

I said, voice low and laced with anger, "Why aren't you pregnant?"

Laurie was out of options. "You don't want to know the real story. And yes, I remember the three of you."

We didn't move, eyes on her.

"I remember everybody." She fixed her hair. "So what do you want? An apology? Okay. I'm sorry."

Cristina bit back with, "Not good enough."

Laurie was about to say something more but hesitated. She fought back a tear. "These people—they set me up, just like you. I crashed into them, but I couldn't afford to pay. So this is how I pay them back."

"Hold it. Pay them back?" I asked.

"The accidents. They aren't real. They're staged."

I felt a rush of equal parts happiness and anger.

"I feel terrible, okay? But I don't have family—no rich uncle to bail me out. I fake everything for them so they can get the money." She let out a long sigh. "They say I only have to help them with two more stages. Then I'm free."

The three of us shared a look of shock.

"The driver and the others are bad people." Laurie looked at me. "Take my advice and stay away. Just move on with your life. Go back to Canada." She turned to leave.

Was she joking? "How can you say that?" I asked. "You're taking advantage of innocent people. It's dangerous, and one of these days someone's going to get killed. And then you'll wish you had done something to stop it."

Chapter Six

The rays from the setting sun warmed the condo balcony. Drinks and leftover chips and vegetables with dip littered the table between my grandparents and me.

I tilted back my cup, searching for the last drops of pear juice. Just ice cubes, so I crunched on them. "So not only did she admit to everything, but she refused to do anything about it."

"That's terrible," my grandmother said. "How does she sleep at night?"

"I don't think she cares about other people, Granny."

My grandfather shook his head. "I still can't believe that entire evening was staged. They caused the accident. They ruined our night, and they could've really hurt us."

"We told her all that. She didn't seem to care. And listen to this. I went online, and it turns out accidents like this are big business. This is a huge problem around the world."

"They're criminals," my grandmother said.

"Yes. They damaged my car and took my money," said Grandpa John. "And the worst part is, they made us feel horrible about it."

"They even have a catchy name for it," I said. "Crash for cash."

"What a terrible thing! People will stop at nothing for money," my grandmother said.

We caught the tail end of the sunset, then packed everything up and headed inside. I helped with the dishes, and when the doorbell rang my grandfather let Ruby and Cristina in. I made the introductions and grabbed my purse.

"I was just telling my grandparents that the accident was not my fault. Or yours, Cristina."

She nodded. "So we're going out to celebrate that. We found the truth, only there's not much we can do about it. We might as well have some fun!"

"All dressed up." My grandfather smiled. "What's the plan?"

"Well, being the local girl," Cristina said, "I'm taking them to an authentic

Coachella Valley celebration. We're going to glamtastic Palm Springs for its Thursday night Village Fest."

"Oh, that's fun. Maya, leave your cell on, and don't stay out too late."

With the roof down and the music up, we drove in Cristina's silver VW Jetta.

From the backseat, Ruby shouted, "What's Village Fest?"

"It's a fantastic street fair where you can shop, eat and dance your heart out," Cristina explained as we drove through the descending darkness. "You'll soon see that Palm Springs is the real desert experience."

"Because?" I asked.

"There are fewer snowbirds and retired people. It's more hip."

Ruby leaned forward. "Are we hipsters?"

Cristina took the Palm Springs exit. "We sure are!"

The moment we entered the city, the number of people and cars overwhelmed me. It took a few laps around the block to find a parking spot. Outside the car, Cristina grabbed our hands, and we stood in a tight circle on the sidewalk.

"Friends from NYC and Vancouver. We are gathered tonight for one thing, and one thing only. After all we've been through…after our newfound friend-ship…it's time to celebrate. *¿Estás listo para divertirse.*"

Ruby and I looked at her.

"Spanish for 'Are you ready to have fun?'"

"How do I look?" asked Ruby.

"Perfect," I said. "Yes, we are ready! Let's go!"

We broke our circle and followed Cristina. We weaved past cars and people onto a very jammed Palm Canyon Drive. The palm-tree-lined road was bumper-to-bumper with people.

Our first stop was dinner. Cristina stopped at a food truck. "So this place is my favorite."

Tropical Flame 'N' Grill was scrawled on the side of the truck in bright blues, reds and yellows.

Ruby asked, "What do you get here?"

"Everything's good. But I usually order the cha-cha chicken."

Minutes later I was staring down at a bowl of chicken with black beans, brown rice and slaw. "This looks so good!"

"Tastes better! And wait till you see dessert," Cristina said before taking a big bite.

I dug in. "Tastes incredible!"

"I'm sorry that your holidays were ruined by what happened."

"It's okay. I've been here lots. It was just bad luck. I still like it here."

"Well, I brought you here to show you that there's another side to the condos and golf courses."

I took another big bite, despite being stuffed. Why? Why not!

"There's crime everywhere," Ruby said. "And I've seen a lot of it living in New York. And my guess is, there are even more of these crash-for-cash scams there. So please don't think we don't like it here."

"All right. Ready to do some shopping?" Cristina asked.

We followed her along the busy road, weaving around the throngs of people fighting to get a look at the booths. Our first stop was the booth of a woman who made jewelry. The prices were good, so I had to pick a bracelet up for myself, my mom and my grandmother.

"Big spender!" Ruby joked.

"You gotta get gifts for home, right?"

"True."

Cristina said, "Well, there's tons more."

We stopped at a booth full of well-priced silk scarves. A few steps away a magician was doing card tricks. Then there was a guy who made wood chimes. My dad loved those, so I picked one up for him. We were only half a block up the first section, and my feet were sore. And I had spent most of my cash.

Cristina asked, "Ready for our first dessert? Because it's right over there."

A man stood in front of a row of six tall, bright flames that rose out of small cylinders. The entire thing was encased in glass. He placed ten extra-large marshmallows on a stick and held it toward the flames until they were perfectly toasted.

We took turns pulling them off the stick.

"So?" Cristina asked.

"Awesome," Ruby said.

"Yes. Perfectly messy."

The dessert became a game, trying to eat the marshmallows before they fell off the stick.

I licked my fingers. "So this might sound like a strange thing to ask, but are you guys a little worried about Laurie? Or is it just me?"

"What do you mean?" Cristina asked.

"Well, she might be involved, but she wasn't the one behind the wheel."

Ruby added, "She did say she was trapped by those guys."

"Right. Kind of like us, but without a grandfather—"

Cristina cut in. "Or a parent to help bail us out."

"Yeah," Ruby agreed. "But she did refuse to help us. So why should we help her?"

I nodded. "True. And what can we really do now anyway?"

The conversation left us without answers, so we kept moving. After downing some freshly squeezed lemonade, we stopped at a store with lots of Palm Springs memorabilia. Ruby clapped her hands, excited to pick up some gifts to take home. We gathered around a mirror near a selection of hats and had fun trying them all on.

Between a row of T-shirts and snow globes, I noticed a man watching us. He had on a stars-and-stripes tank top. I whispered, "There's a disgusting guy checking us out. Can we leave?"

The girls agreed, and we were soon back in the safety of the massive crowds. A man dressed as Elvis caught our attention, a large crowd gathering around him as he sang.

Cristina started to dance, pulling Ruby and me in. She twirled me around.

In the blur of spectators I spotted the guy from the store again.

I kept smiling as I spoke to the girls, so as not to tip him off. "That weirdo is following us."

Cristina took the lead, and we broke off dancing and folded back into the crowd.

Moving quickly past pedestrians, I looked over my shoulder. Stars-and-Stripes was catching up. Our celebration night was quickly turning into an escape from stranger danger. My heart raced, fueled by our fast pace and nerves. Suddenly the crowd of strangers felt less comforting. "Where are we going, Cristina?"

She pointed. "There."

Ahead was a large collection of paintings on tall pedestals. There was everything from landscapes to abstracts.

We pushed through shoppers until we were surrounded by paintings. Out of breath, I asked, "What now?"

"Hide!" Cristina ordered.

I scrunched up beside a painting of a large red flower. Behind it were thousands of different-sized interconnecting circles. Staring at the pattern, it looked like they were changing shape between big and small.

I leaned forward just past the edge of the painting and scanned the faces of the crowd until I found the man in the stars and stripes. He was looking in every direction, like he had lost something. That's when I recognized him. He was the tow-truck driver from the night of the accident.

Chapter Seven

We had immediately called it a night and made it home without any more drama. After tossing and turning all night, I awoke the next morning more confused than ever. Why would that guy want to follow us? And how did he find us, and what did he want with us?

Cristina picked us up, and we went back to the Beach Cove Café. Javier was not pleased when he learned we had gone to see Laurie. When he heard that we were followed by one of the guys from the night of my accident, he slammed the folder of receipts he was carrying down onto the table.

I was hoping he'd offer us a smoothie and a hamburger for our hard work. I guess that wasn't realistic.

"You shouldn't have done that, Cristina."

"But it wasn't my fault we were followed," she whined.

"You don't get it. You were followed *because* you went to see Laurie. She tipped them off."

"Why don't we all have a smoothie and calm down?" My comment fell on deaf ears.

"Your safety is what I care about. You're dealing with a network of people who are staging accidents. That's criminal."

"So we should go to the police?"

Javier didn't answer. Cristina turned to us. "All I wanted was a fun night out. I wasn't looking for trouble."

Javier picked up the folder. "In journalism class, we call where you're at a 'crossroads.' You have information that may put more people in danger if you *don't* act on it. If you *do* act, you could put yourselves in further danger."

"What should we do?" Cristina asked.

"The three of you need to handle this now in a legit way. If you go to the police, you need solid evidence. You need an investigative journalist to get that."

"Aren't *you* one of those?" I asked.

He nodded. "Here's the deal. If I help you, we do it my way."

We all nodded. I let out a small cheer.

"And I'm going to write an article for my class. Who knows—maybe it'll even get published." He stood up. "I get off work in an hour. Until then your task is to think about our next lead."

"Already ahead of you," Ruby said. She turned to her phone and worked on it for a minute while we watched. Then she slid the phone to the middle of the table. There was a photo from the night of my accident. Dale was talking to my grandfather. Ruby reached over and pinched in, revealing the tow truck. A pixelated logo on the side of the truck read *Cactus Towing*.

We all turned to Javier.

"You girls are way too good at this."

With Javier in the lead, I buckled into the back of his convertible Jeep Wrangler. The late-afternoon sun was scorching—I badly needed sunscreen and an icy drink. We approached an industrial area on the edge of town where the road turned into desert. A sign attached to a barbed-wire fence warned us to keep out.

Slowing the jeep, Javier muttered, "Anybody see a sign? I didn't."

I began to wonder what a Canadian girl was doing out here. The secure gates of the condo community, the pool and the tennis courts all seemed very far away.

Ruby had her phone out. She pointed to a sign. The words *Cactus Towing and Salvage* were painted on a wooden cutout of a tow truck. Two old tires hung from large hooks.

Javier said, "It's closed. There's a gate blocking the entrance. I'll do a drive around."

I held on to the jeep as he drove down an uneven path along the perimeter of the property. To my right the fence continued. To my left the endless desert stretched out as far as I could see—a no-man's-land.

Javier slowed the jeep and pulled alongside the fence, almost touching it. I followed his lead and got out.

"This fence goes on forever. What now?" Cristina asked.

"I'd like to see what's on the other side of that." Javier peered through the fence at the rows of old cars and mountain-high piles of metal parts spread over the lot. "I need to take a closer look."

Javier returned to his jeep and stood on the front passenger seat to peer over the fence. He waved us up.

In the jeep, I pulled myself up using the sturdy rollover bar. Javier stepped back down. Ruby said, "I'm coming."

"Someone has to stay here." Before anyone could offer, he threw his keys to Cristina. "Any trouble, take off, and we'll meet up somewhere else."

"Okay," said Cristina.

I followed Javier, extending my arms to the top of the fence, my feet balanced on the roll bar of the jeep. I took a breath and then placed a foot onto the fence. Carefully holding my balance, I moved the next foot over. Javier hit the ground and survived the fall, so I gave it a try. Up and over, I grasped the other side of the fence. My fingers were slowly giving in to the pain. I pushed back and let go. My landing was hard and dusty, but I was in one piece.

After Ruby made it over, we headed out, keeping close to Javier.

Endless rows of rusted cars lay before us. Some were sandwiched ten high, while others had their hoods up, guts exposed.

I crept along, keeping low like Javier. Behind me, Ruby filmed our adventure.

Stepping past a car that had its fender and windshield crushed, I heard a loud growling noise. I jumped and let out a small scream.

The sound of guard dogs barking sent us racing to the protection of a flattened school bus. Javier pulled Ruby and me onto the roof.

"Where are they?" Ruby cried out.

"I hate dogs!" I exclaimed. "I'm more of a cat person."

Javier didn't acknowledge my joke, scanning the area while I lay down on my stomach. "I don't see them."

"I don't want to see them," I said. "We need to get back to Cristina." I looked at Ruby. "Right?"

"We came all the way out here. Let's find some evidence first," she said.

The barking stopped, and Javier climbed down. He walked cautiously around, scoping out the area for us. "Think it's clear," he called up.

I followed Ruby down. I didn't see any guard dogs. "Maybe they're on leashes."

A car caught my eye. I moved toward it for a closer look. "This is the car I smacked into that night."

Ruby got it on her camera. "I think the license plates have changed. Instead of California, now they're Arizona. That's something, right?"

Javier nodded. "Not much else to see around here. Let's go."

"What about that?" Ruby asked, motioning to a trailer up on cement blocks.

We approached it, and the loud barking started up again.

Javier pointed, "Look, the sound is coming from a set of speakers."

"So there are no dogs?" I asked.

"Nope. Just cheap security."

I smiled. "Then let's go inside."

"Good idea," agreed Ruby.

"Terrible idea, actually," said Javier. "It's time to go. I'll try to run the plates. It's a great start."

As I turned to follow him out, the door to the trailer screeched open. An older man, clearly annoyed, held up a baseball bat.

"We're closed! How'd you get in here?"

I turned to Javier, ready to run for it.

Chapter Eight

The man stepped out of the trailer and raised his bat. "How'd you get in?"

Ruby and I huddled close to Javier.

"We're lost," he said.

The man said, "Can't you see we're closed? And that means you're trespassing." He took another step forward, and the loud, angry barking started again.

He moved to the speakers and flicked them off.

I wanted to ask him questions, but we were trapped on his property. Besides, he didn't seem in the mood. Plus, he had that baseball bat.

Javier lifted his arms, trying to make it clear he wasn't interested in fighting. "We're sorry. We shouldn't have come in here. We'll be on our way."

The man looked over at me, squinting his eyes as if to see me better. Then he pointed with the bat at Ruby. "Why is she recording me?"

Javier grabbed Ruby's phone and stuffed it into his pocket. "Kids these days...always with the selfies. Sorry again. I'm just trying to get these girls back home." Whatever headway Javier had made with the man was gone now.

"Still don't see what you're doing in here. How'd you 'wander' in here over the fence?"

The three of us stood there, out of excuses.

"So you admit that you are trespassing then?"

Javier nodded. "We're very sorry. We'll walk away right now and you'll never see us again."

"And I won't charge you with trespassing."

I was going back to Vancouver soon. This was my one and only opportunity to get an answer to a question that had plagued my entire vacation. I stepped forward. "More like we won't have you charged with crashing-for-cash scams. The car that hit me is right over there."

"What are you talking about? There's no scam here," he said, motioning again with his bat, clearly wanting us to leave.

Javier put his hand on my arm. "Maya, please stop."

"It's an insurance scam," I continued.

"What in the world?" The man seemed genuinely confused.

"If I'm wrong, then why does that car have new plates?" I pointed.

"We get all types of cars from all over the United States in here. That's why it's called a towing company." He turned away and back again. "Why should I have to explain my business to *you*—a total stranger on *my* property?"

"Because I smashed into that car! And there was a pregnant lady inside who wasn't really pregnant!" I took a deep breath. "And someone who works for Cactus Towing has been following us."

The man chuckled. "Really? You weave quite the story. I don't want to be the one to state the obvious"— he touched his temple—"but you've clearly got problems."

He stood there, the baseball bat now resting on his shoulder. "And I'm beginning to think I might charge you all for being on my property after all."

Javier tried to pull me away, but Ruby stepped in.

"Great idea. Let's get the police over here. We have proof. All we have to do is tell them about Laurie."

"Who's Laurie? This another story you're cooking up? Now I know the heat's gotten to your heads." He turned to Javier. "I'm going to give you one minute to get these nut jobs off my land."

"We're going," said Javier. "Thank you, thank you." He pulled us around the corner and back to the fence.

Cristina jumped up and down when she saw us. She hugged each of us as we scrambled up and over. "You're all alive! I thought those dogs ate you!"

"They weren't real." I tried to explain, but she had a hard time believing me. "Cristina, it was awesome. We found the car that hit us, just sitting there with new plates."

"What?"

Ruby jumped in. "And we talked to a man who came at us with a baseball bat! You should've seen Maya—"

"I accused him of doing crash for cash. He's got a thousand cars to do it with and—"

"Stop it!" said Javier. "You screwed it all up, and we were lucky to get out of there. Why did you tell him every-thing? Now they can just cover it all up. There's no story here. It's over."

Javier got in the jeep, slammed his door and didn't speak to me the entire way home.

The tennis ball flew over the net, past the out-of-bounds line and wedged itself in the chain-link fence.

"I think that's out." Ruby turned to pluck the ball free.

I smiled at her sarcastic comment and returned to the baseline to receive her serve.

Not that I was into the game at all. Javier was no longer willing to help us out. He blamed me for ruining everything. I think he was more upset about not getting to write his article than about not getting any kind of justice.

"You ready?" Ruby called out from crosscourt.

My grandparents, worried about me obsessing over the accident, were happy I was out here. *You're ruining what's left of your vacation over something that wasn't your fault*, they'd said.

The ball whizzed past me.

"I wasn't ready, Ruby!"

"Sorry! Want to quit?"

"No, I guess not." I picked the ball up and lobbed it over. I could never have predicted how this vacation would turn out. I remembered how happy I'd been sitting in my seat at the Indian Wells tennis tournament. And then it had all gone sideways.

Ruby returned the ball, and I smacked it as hard as I could, venting my leftover anger and frustration.

How many other people were getting scammed somewhere right now? It was bad enough that I'd gotten pulled into the mess. But it was worse that I had had an opportunity to stop these people. And I'd blown it.

The ball landed at my baseline, and I turned sideways, slapping it with a backhander.

I had yet to figure out how to pay back my grandparents. I knew I would have to fight to get them to accept any money from me, but it was the right thing to do. Never thought I'd return from an all-expenses-paid vacation with a monster debt instead of a couple of T-shirts and a snow globe of Chino Canyon.

Ruby hit a beautiful slice serve and I watched it clear the net, smothered in backspin. I half ran to the net and just got the edge of my racket on it and flopped it over.

The ball landed without much bounce, and Ruby couldn't get to it.

"Nice one," she said.

We met at the net.

"Think I'm done for the day," I said.

Ruby nodded.

"Want to hear something sad?" I asked.

"Not really."

"Tonight I have to go online to choose my seat for the flight home."

"Thanks for the depressing news. I'd forgotten the break was almost over. I'm going to miss the blue skies."

"The swimming pools. And the palm trees," I added.

"The green, green grass," Ruby said.

"And the wind farms," I said.

"Really?" Ruby asked.

"I think they're cool."

"Oh, eating outside at night."

"Yeah," I said. "I love that. And the smoothies at the Beach Cove Café."

"Cristina." Ruby sighed.

"Yes…and you."

"Aww!" Ruby leaned over the net and gave me a hug.

I helped round up the tennis balls and then headed to the condo. My plan was simple. Spend the night with my grandparents. Watch the sun go down and maybe some TV.

"Maya?" my grandmother called out.

"Yeah, it's me. Hi." I found her outside on the balcony and gave her a kiss.

"There's someone on the phone for you."

"For me? Who is it?"

"I'm not sure. She called twice while you were out."

I took the phone. "Hello?"

"Hi. It's me. Laurie. Can we meet up? I need to see you."

Chapter Nine

Laurie stood on the other side of the security gate.

"How'd you find me?" I asked.

"On the night of the accident your grandfather exchanged information with Dale."

Ruby said, "Dale was the guy in the car with you."

Laurie nodded. "He's the brains behind the scam. He has access to a lot full of old cars, vans and pickups to choose from. He's the man who thinks he owns me." She checked left and right behind her. "Can I come in?"

I looked at Laurie, standing exposed to the world while I was protected on this side of the gate. I punched the code into the keypad, and the gate buzzed unlocked.

Laurie checked behind her again before entering. Then she headed for a spot in the shade and sat down, looking around in wonder. "This place is nice. Real upscale."

"Why exactly are you here?" Ruby said, getting right to the point.

"Because of what you said. About doing the right thing."

I looked at Laurie's hands. They were shaking.

"You feel bad, I get it," replied Ruby. "But you're still hurting people."

"Do you think I want to?" Laurie wiped away a tear. "I'm not like that."

I stood above her, arms crossed, trying to decide if this was all an act.

Laurie started to stand up. "This was a mistake. I should go."

"You came here to tell us something," I said coldly. "So tell us."

She nodded, sitting back down. "I thought that if you knew more about my story, maybe you'd understand."

"Okay," I said. "Spill."

"I'm from a small town. Stanford. Illinois. Like so many others, my dream, ever since I was a kid, was to be an actress. There was zero opportunity back home for something like that, so as soon as I'd saved enough, I bought a beat-up old car and headed west to Los Angeles. But I had only been in California for a couple of days when I hit those guys' car, just like you did, and, well, I think you know the rest."

"Keep talking."

Laurie's eyes welled with tears. Her hands were still shaking. "Like I told you when you found me, I couldn't afford to pay them for the damage. I had to work it off. They keep saying my debt is nearly paid, but I don't think it ever will be. And I can't take it anymore."

"So you want our help," Ruby said. "Just one question. How come you sent that guy after us?"

"What are you talking about? What guy?"

"The tow-truck driver. He was following us when we were in Palm Springs."

"Are you sure?"

I said, "Yes."

Laurie stood up again, clearly agitated. "I'm sorry I bothered you.

Just pretend I was never here," she said, looking around nervously.

She headed to the gate, but I blocked her way.

"What's going on?" I asked. "What changed your mind just now?"

"These guys don't mess around," said Laurie.

"Yeah," Ruby said, "you told us that. But they have to be stopped."

I had an idea. Something that might make Laurie more likely to cooperate with us. "We know a newspaper reporter. He's already offered to help us out."

"A real newspaper reporter?"

"Uh-huh," I said. Ruby glanced at me, but I kept my poker face. *Reporter* sounded way better than *journalism student*.

Laurie paused for a moment, then nodded. "Okay. It's happening again tonight. They're staging an accident."

"Perfect," Ruby said. "We can get it on camera and expose them."

"Your reporter won't mind doing this?"

"No, he's always looking for a good story."

"How do you know him? Neither of you live here."

I took the lead. "We know his assistant, Cristina." What was one more lie?

"Well, if you're sure this will work..." Laurie said, wringing her hands.

"We're sure," I said. Okay, two lies.

Laurie gave us the details of the staging before she sneaked away. Ruby and I met up at the pool and called Cristina to outline the plan.

I told my grandparents I was going to the movies. Not a total lie. We were going to be down at the cinema, but there wouldn't be any popcorn, extra butter and iced tea tonight. I stood, one hand on a palm tree, outside the cinema parking lot.

Ruby waved at me from the opposite side of the street. We wanted to record all angles. She called out, one hand on her phone and the left cupping her mouth, "No sign of Cristina and Javier."

I shook my head, knowing I had double-checked that this was the right spot. Then I spotted a car, the lead car. It stopped and idled at the side of the road. I could see a woman in the front passenger seat. It was Laurie, probably in that pregnancy costume.

As if on cue, a tow truck appeared to my right. I secured it in the crosshairs of my phone's camera. The words *Cactus Towing* confirmed that Laurie had told us the truth. It was on!

The tow truck kept at a low speed, circling through the parking lot, trolling for young or old drivers coming out of a movie.

A loud clap caught my attention. It was Ruby across the street. I was relieved to see Cristina and Javier at her side. Ruby gave me a thumbs-up, but I was distracted by the tow truck's movements.

It was onto someone. It trailed its prey, a white Toyota sedan. It was unsettling to be on the other side of this scam. Seeing the setup. Knowing that less than a week earlier, I'd been driving the target car. It was an eerie feeling, knowing an accident was about to happen. At least it was the last one these people would ever set up.

I stayed hidden behind the palm tree and kept my phone trained on the Toyota. Inside was an older couple who had no idea they were being watched. They stopped at the exit with their left turn indicator on. As they turned, the tow truck flicked its lights once, obviously signaling the car Dale and Laurie were in. What Dale didn't know was that Javier was about to call 9-1-1.

The car lurched forward and sped up, maneuvering itself in front of the Toyota.

It felt like the night of my accident was replaying, frame by frame. The couple was probably complaining about the terrible driver zooming past them. In the car in front of them, Dale was about to hit the brakes.

I gripped my hands tightly together and called out, "Brace!" as if they could hear me. The red brake lights lit up, and I half turned, my phone still capturing the moment. I scrunched up my eyes at the sound of screeching tires, and then there was silence.

My eyes popped open, but instead of a crash scene, the road was clear. There was no sign of the target or the tow truck. The lead car pulled a U-turn and stopped in front of me. I stood frozen, my phone still aimed and recording as Dale jumped out of the car and rushed toward me. He grabbed me and pulled me into the backseat.

I looked up to see Ruby watching in horror. The force of the car's acceleration pushed me back into the seat, and we were gone.

Chapter Ten

My heart raced as I reached for the door handle and pulled on it, but it wouldn't open.

"Child locks are on," Dale said with a sneer. "So sit back and be quiet."

I tried the door again and again, pulling as hard as I could, praying that somehow the lock would snap and the door would swing open. I wasn't against jumping and rolling to safety. I'd roll the dice for scrapes or broken bones.

Dale said, "And stop whimpering!"

Was I? I also hadn't noticed my heart racing out of control. *Calm down and think*, I ordered myself. As I got my breathing a little under control, I remembered that Laurie was in the passenger seat.

"What's going on?" I called to her, pushing on the seat. "What happened to the plan?"

She didn't say anything, her head aimed forward.

"Wait a minute. This whole thing was your idea? How could we have been so stupid as to trust you?"

Again she didn't say anything.

"Where are you taking me?" I was trying hard not to panic.

Dale slammed his hand against the steering wheel. "I said *shut up*!"

I looked out the window. There was just darkness. I was Palm Springs-experienced enough to know that no sign of lights meant we were somewhere in the desert. I scanned the backseat for anything I could use to break a window or stop the car. There was nothing.

"My friends are going to find me. Laurie, you know who was there. They're probably behind us." I glanced over my shoulder through the dirty back window. Nothing.

"If she doesn't shut up," Dale said to Laurie, "then I'm going to do it for her."

Tears streamed down my face. *Come up with a plan.*

I could kick the back of the driver seat enough to bother Dale. If he got out to yell at me, I could make a run for it.

The tears continued. *Don't give up.*

If this was an old car, maybe I could kick out the window. Then jump through.

I wiped away the tears. *They haven't won yet.*

Another idea surfaced. *Reach around and cover Dale's eyes with your hands. Blind him into swerving off the road. This car doesn't have air bags.* I could brace for the crash, then escape.

A light went off at the back of my brain. I had my phone! There had to be a 9-1-1 option. I flicked up on the lock screen and saw the words *Emergency Dial.* I touched it and hoped the phone would do the rest. I waited, the phone pressed against my left ear so it was blocked from view.

The car slowed and pulled into a long driveway.

Come on, come on. Why isn't it dialing? Then I saw the words *No Service.*

The headlights shut off, and everything went black.

The car stopped, and they got out. My door opened, and Dale grabbed me. I struggled to get loose, but his grip was too tight. He dragged me along a dirt path toward a large building.

I tried to turn—where was Laurie?

Dale kicked the door open and pushed me through a large office area and then through another door.

He released me, and I fell to the floor.

The dimly lit space looked like a car garage—more like a dead-car morgue.

Dale stood above me, pointing. "I saw you together. You think I wouldn't have found out? That you and Laurie would have the brains to take me down? Next time, be a little less obvious when you're trying to film me." He wiped sweat from his forehead. "You should have minded your own business. Moved on with your life."

I was too scared to move. I swallowed hard, muttering, "My friends are coming for me."

"No one's coming for you! No one's going to find you!" He turned and slammed the door behind him. I heard the *click* of the lock.

After a few minutes I got to my feet and looked around, feeling like a scared rat. Where was I? An old sports car sat in the middle of the room, its hood up, no engine.

Other than a few tools, car rims and half-naked chicks taped to the wall, I was alone.

Best vacation ever.

I heard footsteps outside the door and quickly grabbed a wrench, hiding it behind my back.

The door scraped open and Dale appeared. Behind him was Laurie, tears streaming down her face.

I took a step to the side, eyeing the open door. Could I make it? I squeezed the wrench. Could I take him?

Dale grabbed Laurie's arm. "Turning on me was the dumbest move of your stupid life." He pushed her toward me, and she cried out.

"You two deserve each other." Then he was out the door again.

Laurie's hands covered her face. She just stood there, muttering to herself.

Was she praying?

After a moment she lifted her head and screamed, "I wish I'd never met you!"

"How is this *my* fault? We trusted you. You are a liar!"

"I meant Dale! But the same goes for you."

"What did *I* do? Except believe that you actually wanted to stop them."

"Are you kidding me? Do you think I set this up? I warned you that Dale was smart. He found out. He's been following us since you showed up at the clothing store!"

Oh. "So you didn't set me up?" I asked, feeling a bit sheepish.

"No! I stuck to the plan. But they already knew."

There was silence.

"Now what?" I asked finally.

"You said your friends are coming—"

"You believed me? How would they ever find me? If they'd followed us, they would've been here by now."

Laurie ran her fingers through her hair. "I'm scared to think what Dale is going to do to us."

More silence.

I moved around the room some more. There was a rusty-looking shelf that ran about halfway up the far wall. I put my foot on the first level to test its stability. So far, so good.

"What are you doing?" Laurie asked.

No idea. I kept climbing and pushed some boxes to the side. There it was, our exit plan. "Laurie, come here!"

I climbed back down and showed her. "We have to pull this shelf out from the wall. There's a window behind it."

"Really? Okay."

"First we need to take everything off the shelf."

We started with the first row, and then I climbed back up to hand Laurie the rest. The next step was to slide the shelf far enough away from the wall that we could access the window.

"Laurie, can you cough for me? It will cover the sound."

She nodded and coughed on cue as I pulled on the shelving structure. It made a terrible scraping sound against the cement floor. It didn't move much over her three coughs, but just enough.

We heard distant voices on the other side of the building.

"We have to move quickly. Like, now."

I moved behind the shelf and climbed up to the window. "It won't budge."

"Here, let me try," said Laurie, climbing up beside me and giving it a good push.

The window would not open.

Chapter Eleven

The window was sealed tightly from years of never being used. "Maybe if we try together," I suggested. "Ready?"

Laurie nodded.

"Pull!"

I felt it give a tiny bit. "Again," I said, my muscles straining to their max. The window started to lift.

"Oh my god, it's so heavy!" exclaimed Laurie.

It took both of us to get it high enough to get through. But in our excitement, we let go, and it crashed back down.

The distant voices stopped.

"We have to hurry!" said Laurie.

"We need something to prop it open. Something about the height of a racket handle." I looked around briefly but heard the voices start up again—no doubt Dale and his friends were on their way to investigate.

"What should we do?" said Laurie, more panicked than ever.

"Try again." It took all of our energy to pull the window back up.

"Maya, I can't hold this for much longer."

Executive decision time, I thought. I couldn't hold on much longer either.

And one of us getting out was better than none. I looked at Laurie. "You first."

"No. We go together. And you can't hold the window alone."

"Laurie, it's time. Go, *now!*"

Laurie sighed and let go of the window. I took all its weight. As she got her first leg through, I felt the strain in my fingers first. Then it traveled quickly up my arms. *Steady now.*

Behind me the voices grew louder, angrier.

Laurie was through, looking up at me from the outside.

I could hear the voices right outside the door. It was too late.

"What are you waiting for, Maya?"

"I can't get through without getting crushed. Go get help!" I stepped back and let go.

I scrambled down and turned to the door as it opened. I was expecting Dale, but it was the old man from Cactus Towing.

"What is that racket? Oh, it's you again," he grumbled, trusty baseball bat in hand.

Whatever trouble I had been in before, it had just doubled.

"Come here!" he commanded.

All the exits were blocked. All I could think of was my grandparents. And my parents. They had trusted me to follow rules and stay out of trouble. I had done the exact opposite, starting with talking to strangers.

I could apologize, but that wouldn't do any good. I could try begging.

The old man turned from me to the two men who'd followed him—Dale and, behind him, the tow-truck driver. "What's going on here, boys?"

Dale spoke first. "Nothing, Pops, just hanging out. Thought we'd have some fun."

Pops?

The old man looked back at me. I may have glared a bit. "Doesn't seem to me like she's having much fun."

Was that a serious comment or sarcasm? Dale's face was expressionless.

"And you, Joe? What's your story?"

"I was out driving the truck," said the tow-truck driver. "Business was slow, so I came back and just found Dale in here with her. Where's the other one?"

"I'm not buying it," said the old man. "Wait a minute. There's another one?"

Dale jumped in. "Shut up, Joe! You know that's a lie."

"No, it's true, Pops. Like I said, I was driving the truck."

The old man pointed the baseball bat at me. "This little one was snooping around here before. I already warned you to stay off my property."

"I know I shouldn't have. I'm so…" I didn't know what to say. The last thing I wanted was to anger this guy any more.

"And boys, you know what she accused me of?"

Dale and Joe said, "What?" at the same time.

"She told me that I was involved in some sort of crash-for-cash scam."

"Sir, I didn't know what I was saying. Please forgive me for being so rude." I was begging now.

"I raised these boys alone, as best as I could. This wrecking yard is a family business. The boys work it, and one day it's all supposed to go to them. It's not easy making a living these days," he continued. "The tow truck does okay, the car parts less so. But we work hard and do the best we can."

While he rambled, I kept praying Laurie had found some help.

"So, boys, what I can't figure out is why she would say something like that."

They both laughed clearly fake laughs.

"No way," said Dale. "Right, Joe?"

Joe shook his head. "First I heard of it."

This was not going well. I had to get out of there. "Why don't I leave so you can figure all this out?"

"Oh no you don't," said the old man. "I want to sort this out *now*. When you came by with your friends—what's your name?"

"Maya," I answered.

The old man moved slowly, favoring one leg in particular. For the first time, I clued in on his having an injury. He turned to the boys. "So when Maya here comes by and accuses me of setting up crashes for money, I assumed she had the wrong place." He found a chair to sit in. "But what she said really bothered me. It stayed with me. So I looked around a little."

What did he mean? I wondered.

"It hasn't been easy being off work. Getting old just isn't any fun. The arms and legs stop cooperating. Luckily, I have my boys. Maya, do you mind stepping closer?"

I took a few nervous steps toward him.

"On behalf of my sons, I want to apologize for what they've done to you."

Both boys jumped forward in protest, but the old man shouted at them to shut up and sit down.

I smiled for the first time. Now *their* escape was blocked.

"What they've done is not only wrong, but also horribly illegal. I'm ashamed. My name's Jerry. We need to get you back home—"

Just then the door flew open behind him. Javier, Cristina and Ruby stormed inside, followed by Laurie.

Ruby, Cristina and Laurie stayed by the door while Javier strode toward Jerry, shouting, "Stay away from her!"

I put my hands out, palms up. "Javier, it's—"

"I got this, Maya." He turned to Jerry. "You're using the cars in this place to run an auto scam."

Jerry nodded. "Yes. I know."

"And I called the police. They're on their way."

"Good. Thank you."

"And I'm writing an article, and everyone will know."

"Okay."

"Too bad—" Javier stopped, surprised. "Wait. What did you say?"

Sirens blared in the distance.

Jerry said, "I would've called the police too." He looked at his sons. "They've made a terrible mistake and will have to face the consequences."

Dale and Joe sat, heads slumped. Their fates were sealed.

Suddenly Ruby and Cristina had their arms around me, and everyone was talking at once. I felt the tension flush out of my body. I was going to be okay.

"You know what I could go for right now?" I asked, smiling. "One of those smoothies from the Beach Cove Café."

Chapter Twelve

It felt great to be back on the court.

I tossed the ball with my racket and smashed it over the net and deep into the blue court.

Ruby was quick with a big swing, followed by a loud grunt. The ball barreled at me, hit the ground and lurched forward. I barely got any racket on it, and my return collapsed into the net.

"Nice return, Ruby! You had too much top spin on it for me."

She called out from the other side of the court, "Thanks!"

We continued to play even though we both knew our time together was nearly up. While it felt great to be back to spending half my day at the pool and the other half on the courts, it was time to go home. And I missed home. My regular old boring life was fine with me.

"One last one?" Ruby asked.

"Okay."

Her serve came in fast and low over the net, and it took all my arm strength on the backhand to return it. Deep into a barrage of back-and-forth, I undercut a shot to land just over the net. Ruby ran for it and managed to flip the ball back onto my side. I was already in a full-sprint attack on the net, assuming she'd get it. I extended the tip of my racket but couldn't get to it in time. As the ball landed I hit a half volley, deflecting the ball over.

Ruby kindly lobbed the ball, giving me enough time to get into position.

I faked an overhead slam and did another drop shot. She returned to the net, and we volleyed the ball back and forth until the heat and laughter got the better of us.

Sitting on the bench next to Ruby, chugging down some water, I said, "Best game—"

"Ever," she finished.

We walked and talked all the way back to my grandparents' condo. It didn't feel right to say goodbye just yet, so Ruby came upstairs to hang out a bit more. After a quick shower, I packed the last of my clothes. Heading into the TV room, I was surprised to see Cristina and Javier in there with Ruby.

My grandmother said, "They were just telling us about all your brave efforts."

Javier handed me a rolled-up newspaper.

"Is this it?" I asked, excited.

"Yes."

I unrolled that day's edition of the *Desert Daily News*. The title of Javier's article stretched across the front cover—*Desert Slam*.

Ruby sat next to me to read the two-page article. At the end, there was a small headshot of Javier after his name.

"Congratulations! This is awesome."

"Thank you. I'm actually published. I couldn't have done it if you hadn't pushed me."

"You're an amazing writer."

"I actually think you make a pretty good investigative journalist yourself."

As Javier and Cristina got up to leave, I handed back the paper. "So Dale and Joe have officially been charged?"

"Yes. And the police are doing what they can to find the money they've taken from people." Javier returned the paper to me. "Keep it. This is your copy. I also emailed you the web link."

"Please take it," Cristina said, laughing. "We have lots more in the car!"

Laurie stepped out of the bathroom in new clothes, her hair down. *Relaxed* was the word that came to mind.

She turned to my grandparents. "Thank you so much for letting me stay here."

They exchanged hugs.

"I hate to crash the party," my grandmother said, "but Maya has a plane to catch."

"Yes," Laurie said. "And I should be going too."

I grabbed my suitcase and rolled it to the front door.

In the parking lot, Laurie tossed her bag into the trunk of a beat-up red car with a blue fender and hood. Jerry had provided the car, along with a first repayment of money to her. She stood with the front door open. "It's not much, but it'll get me to Hollywood!"

I waved goodbye and watched her disappear around the corner. She was finally continuing her journey, her dream to go to Los Angeles and become an actress. I really hoped it worked out for her.

"Here we go," I said.

Cristina gave me a big hug. "See you online."

"Yes." I tried to fight back the tears. Then I turned to Ruby, and it all came out.

Ruby held me tightly. "Thanks for making my vacation…interesting."

Everyone laughed, and suddenly it was my turn to get into a car and drive off.

Outside the main gates and on the open road, my grandfather asked, "You doing okay?"

"Actually…do we have time for a stop at the Beach Cove Café?"

He looked at me and smiled.

At the airport, I checked in and chugged the rest of my smoothie before going through security. It was perfect. On the escalator to the gates, I soaked up one last view of the palm trees and inhaled one more big breath of the clean desert air.

At the gate I pulled out the *Desert Daily News* from my backpack and read the article again. I smiled, thinking of all the unexpected good that had come from this trip. Was I actually responsible for this front-page article? I thought about what Javier had said. I had never imagined becoming an investigative journalist.

But I liked the way it sounded. Maybe after I'd won a couple of Grand Slams.

Author's Note

When I was 21, I moved to Los Angeles with a friend. On my first morning in the city, we drove to Beverly Hills. As I pulled into a parking lot, another car appeared out of nowhere, the driver apparently after the same spot I was clearly aiming for. Our cars collided. Even in my panic I remember thinking that the collision seemed staged. I couldn't help but wonder: Was it on purpose? Had she seen that I was a young driver? One thing for sure was, there was no missing my red sports car with its out-of-country plates. When I contacted my insurance company, I was surprised to learn that the other driver reported that she had been badly injured. She had given no indication of this at the scene. Since we had her name and address, my friend and I decided to investigate. We saw her—gardening in her front yard and looking totally fine. Somehow, she still managed to receive a settlement for a lot of money from my insurance company. These days, this kind of scam has a name: crash for cash.

Acknowledgments

Thank you to Eric Walters for taking the time to help me with this project. I greatly appreciate your encouraging words, writing career advice and guidance.

Thank you to my editor, Tanya Trafford. Your expertise was invaluable when helping to craft the characters and story. Your keen eye for detail helped to elevate this book into something I am very proud of.

I am incredibly grateful to my wife. Naomi, you're a well-read, inspirational teacher with a great ability to bring out the best in my writing. You expect nothing but the best from me.

And finally to my niece, Maya. Sorry it took this long to get your name into one of my books. You're the head-liner in this one. This character is based on you—courageous, smart and athletic.

This is my first book in the Orca Soundings series. I hope you enjoy it.

Steven Barwin leads a double life as a writer and a teacher. He is the author of a number of sport-themed books, including the Orca Sports titles *Hardball* and *Hurricane Heat*. He has also written for numerous television shows and contributed to the creation of the NASCAR and World Wrestling DVD board games. Steven lives in Toronto, Ontario, with his family. For more information, please visit www.stevenbarwin.com.